I would like to thank Edmund Jacoby, who gave me the right idea at the perfect time. Many thanks also to tall Robert and small Johanna for our wonderful life together!

Lilli L'Arronge, Münster, 2013

Published in North America in 2017 by Owlkids Books Inc.

Published in Germany under the title *Ich Große — du klein* in 2014 by Verlagshaus Jacoby & Stuart

Published in Canada by
Owlkids Books Inc.
10 Lower Spadina Avenue
Toronto, ON M5V 2Z2

Published in the United States by
Owlkids Books Inc.
1700 Fourth Street
Berkeley, CA 94710

Owlkids Books acknowledges the financial support of the Canada Council for the Arts, the Ontario Arts Council, the Government of Canada through the Canada Book Fund (CBF) and the Government of Ontario through the Ontario Media Development Corporation's Book Initiative for our publishing activities.

Cataloguing data available from Library and Archives Canada

Library of Congress Control Number: 2016946876

ISBN: 978-1-77147-194-7

Edited by: Jessica Burgess and Sarah Howden

ONTARIO ARTS COUNCIL
CONSEIL DES ARTS DE L'ONTARIO
an Ontario government agency
un organisme du gouvernement de l'Ontario

Canada Council
for the Arts

Conseil des Arts
du Canada

Canadä

Manufactured in Dongguan, China, in October 2016, by Toppan Leefung Packaging & Printing (Dongguan) Co., Ltd. Job #BAYDC33

A       B       C       D       E       F

Publisher of Chirp, chickaDEE and OWL
www.owlkidsbooks.com

Owlkids Books is a division of

Bayard
C A N A D A

You and me, as it should be.

You mine   Me yours

You tall  Me small

You smooch

Me kiss

You boo-boo  Me bandage

You: Ouch!   Me: Ouch!

You smarter

Me smart

Okay...   Me: Yes.

You: Yes!   Me: No!

Me cuddle   You cuddlier

You bubble   Me bubblier

Me cool   You cooler

Me wet   You dry

Me neat　You sweet

You shout   Me shush

Me goofy   You goofy too

Me bun   You crumb

Me tired  You wired

Me guide   You scout

Me CHOMP  You chomp

Me romp   You STOMP

You whoop      Me droop

Me pause   You pounce

You bip

Me BOP

You small

Me tall

# ME TALL,
## YOU SMALL

Written and illustrated by
## Lilli L'Arronge

Translated by Madeleine Stratford

## OWLKIDS BOOKS